Sandy

Hannie Truijens

Illustrated by Robert Greary

Chapter 1 Alexander the Great page 3
Chapter 2 First prize for Sandy page 14
Chapter 3 Sandy to the rescue page 22

Nelson

Thomas Nelson and Sons Ltd
Nelson House   Mayfield Road
Walton-on-Thames   Surrey
KT12 5PL   UK

51 York Place
Edinburgh
EH1 3JD   UK

Nelson Blackie
Wester Cleddens Road
Bishopbriggs
Glasgow
G64 2NZ   UK

Thomas Nelson (Hong Kong) Ltd
Toppan Building 10/F
22A Westlands Road
Quarry Bay   Hong Kong

Thomas Nelson Australia
102 Dodds Street
South Melbourne
Victoria 3205   Australia

Nelson Canada
1120 Birchmount Road
Scarborough   Ontario
M1K 5G4   Canada

Text © J.C.M. Truijens 1989
Illustrations © Thomas Nelson & Sons Ltd 1992
Illustrated by Robert Greary

First published by Macmillan Education Ltd 1989

This edition published by Thomas Nelson and Sons Ltd 1992

ISBN 0-17-422496-6
NPN 9 8 7 6 5 4

Printed in China

Chapter 1: Alexander the Great

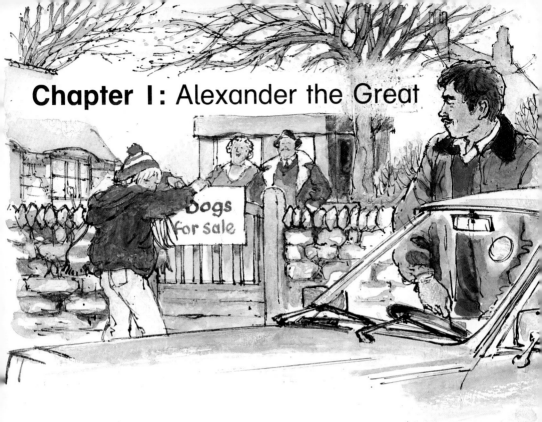

Maggie ran from the car to the farm
gate. Today was a big day for her.
It was her birthday and she was
getting a puppy as a present.
It was her very first dog.

"Can I choose him myself, Dad?" she
asked.

"Yes, of course," said Dad.
"It will be your very own dog and
you must choose the puppy you like best."

It wasn't difficult for Maggie to
choose a puppy.

"This one," she said.
She held up the smallest puppy of the litter.

"He's very clever, I can see it from his face."
Dad went to pay for the puppy and
Maggie carried him to the car.
She had a basket ready for him, and
a puppy biscuit.

The puppy wasn't interested in
the basket or the biscuit.
He sat on Maggie's lap and
licked her hands.

Chris and Mum were waiting at home for Maggie and Dad.

"What an ugly little mongrel," said Chris.

"He's not ugly," said Maggie, "and it doesn't matter that he's a mongrel. He's going to be the best and bravest dog in the world."

"He's sweet," said Mum, "and he's not going to stay little.
Look at his big paws.
He'll grow into a big, strong dog."

"I'm going to call him Alexander the
Great," said Maggie.

"Alexander the Great!" snorted
Chris. "What do you know about
Alexander the Great?"

"I read about him in a book," said Maggie.
"He was a very brave man.
I think it's a good name for my dog."

"I think so too," said Mum, "but
it's a long name."

"I'll call him Sandy for short,"
said Maggie.

That night Sandy slept in Maggie's
room, at the side of her bed.
He started to cry as soon
as Maggie put out the light.
Maggie longed to take him into her bed, but
she had promised Mum that she wouldn't.

"Poor little Sandy," she said.
"Do you miss your mother and
your brothers and sisters?"

Sandy stopped crying as soon as
Maggie spoke to him, so Maggie spent half
the night telling him stories.

Alexander the Great turned out to be a great pest, and that's what Chris called him.

"The Great Pest has been at my football boots again!" he roared.

"He likes them," said Maggie.

"He likes everything," said Chris, "especially if he can chew it."

"He's teething, Chris," said Mum. "He'll get over it."

"But my football boots won't," grumbled Chris.

Maggie usually called her dog Sandy. But when she was angry with him she called him by his full name.

"Alexander the Great," she said as loudly as she could, "DROP that broom and COME HERE."

Sandy was only half listening. He went to Maggie but forgot to drop the broom. CRASH!
Even Mum was angry this time.

"I wish that dog of yours would learn to listen," she said.

9

Sandy really was a pest. He was big and clumsy, and didn't listen very often. Maggie talked to Dad about it.

"How can I make Sandy listen to me, Dad?" she said. "I know he wants to be good but he doesn't know how."

"He's old enough to be trained now," said Dad. "I think we should take him to the training school.
It costs a lot of money, but if you agree it can be your Christmas present."

"Yes please, Dad," said Maggie.

Dad went with Maggie and Sandy for the first time.

"The next time you must go alone with Sandy," said Dad. "He's your dog and he must learn to listen to you."

Sandy tried very hard and learned very quickly. Maggie was very proud of him. After a few lessons he had already learned SIT and HEEL and FETCH.

"You've got a smart dog there," said the trainer.

Sandy and Maggie both agreed.

11

After a few more lessons even Chris
had to agree.

"The Great Pest is learning fast,
Maggie," he said.

"Then stop calling him the Great
Pest," said Maggie. "His name is
Alexander the Great."

But there was one thing that Sandy
couldn't or wouldn't learn.
He couldn't leave cats alone.
He loved to chase them, and wouldn't
come when Maggie called him to heel.

12

Most of all Sandy loved to chase the cat
which lived with the Macdonalds next door.
It was a snooty and silly cat and
was just asking to be chased.
Sandy was always sorry afterwards.

"It's no use looking sorry,"
scolded Maggie. "You must learn not
to chase cats, Sandy.
You have learned everything else,
why can't you learn that?"

Sandy didn't know himself why he
couldn't leave the cat alone.

One day Chris was reading
the newspaper.
He looked up and said to Maggie,
    "There will be a dog show in
town next week. There is also a
prize for the best-trained dog.
Why don't you enter Sandy?"
    "That's a good idea," said Mum,
"Sandy is so well-trained now that he may
win a prize."
    "We'll think about it," said Maggie.

Maggie saved her pocket money and
entered Sandy in the show.
She spent the whole week training him.
He was very good.

"We're going to win the first
prize," said Maggie, "I know we will."

Sandy wagged his tail.
He didn't know what a first prize was, but
if Maggie wanted it he was going to
get it for her.

Soon it was the morning of the dog show. Maggie had brushed Sandy until his coat shone like gold.

The whole family was coming to watch Sandy take the first prize.

It was very busy at the show. There were bulldogs and poodles, spaniels and Great Danes. But there were also some mongrels like Sandy.

"None of them is as clever as you, Sandy," said Maggie proudly.

At last it was Sandy's turn to show what he could do.

Sandy sat when he was told to sit. He came to heel when he was called to heel. He stayed where he was told to stay. He didn't touch the meat on the dish, even though it smelled very good.

Sandy looked up at Maggie proudly. She patted him on the head and said, "You're the best dog in the world."

17

Then something terrible happened.
The snooty, silly cat from next door
jumped up on the wall of the yard.

"Oh, no," said Maggie softly.

"Grrr, Grrr," growled Sandy softly.
He started to walk to the wall.

"SIT," shouted Maggie, but Sandy
wouldn't sit.

"HEEL," shouted Maggie, but Sandy
wouldn't heel.

"STAY," shouted Maggie, but Sandy
ran to the wall.

18

Sandy had spoiled it all.
He was the best-trained dog until
the cat came along.

He wouldn't be getting a prize.
Not a first prize, not a second prize,
not even a third prize.
Poor Sandy. Poor Maggie.

The prizes were handed out.
Maggie and Sandy watched as the red ribbon
was held out to the winning dog.

"That should have been ours," said
Maggie.

19

Sandy looked at Maggie and
then at the red ribbon.
He quickly ran to the front and gently
took the red ribbon out of the lady's hand.
Then he ran back to Maggie and
put it at her feet.

Maggie had tears in her eyes.
"Oh Sandy," she cried,
"th it's not ours, take it back."

Sandy sadly took the ribbon back to
the lady.

Sandy was very quiet for the next
few days. He knew that he had let
Maggie down.

He had bad dreams about a snooty, silly cat.
Maggie had bad dreams about a red ribbon.

Mum tried to cheer Maggie up.

"It was all that cat's fault," she said.

"No, it wasn't," said Maggie.
"It was Sandy's fault.
He just hasn't learnt to leave that cat alone."

Chapter 3: Sandy to the rescue

Weeks went by and Maggie and Sandy had both nearly forgotten the dog show. Maggie kept on training Sandy. She wanted him to listen — even when there were cats around.

Every day it went a little better. And then one day it worked. The cat next door walked past right in front of Sandy.

"HEEL," said Maggie.
Sandy came to Maggie's side and didn't move.

But Sandy wasn't the only dog around that day. The bulldog from down the road had also seen the cat.
The bulldog hadn't been trained at all. He ran after the cat, growling fiercely.

The cat jumped over the fence and ran towards the river.
The bulldog dived under the fence and followed her.

"SIT, HEEL, STAY," shouted Maggie, but the bulldog wouldn't listen to her at all.

23

The cat ran to the bank of the
river and then was trapped.
She climbed up a small tree next to
the river, but it bent under her weight.
She came closer and closer to the water,
and the bulldog stood on the bank and snarled.

The cat couldn't hold on any longer.
She gave one loud mew and fell into the
water.

Maggie and Sandy ran to the bank of
the river. The bulldog growled at
Sandy, turned around, and went home.

Maggie tried to reach out for the
cat, but she was too far out in the river.
Some cats can swim, but this one couldn't.
She went down once and came up again.
She went down a second time and
came up again.

"FETCH," shouted Maggie.
"FETCH THE CAT, SANDY!"

Sandy jumped into the river and
paddled after the cat.
The water was carrying the cat
to a wide bridge.
She went down for the third time.
   "Hurry, hurry," shouted Maggie.
"Get her before she goes under the
bridge."
   Sandy reached the cat just as she
came up for the third time.
He gently gripped her in his mouth, and
then they were both swept under
the bridge.

Maggie wanted to run to the other side of the bridge, but she had to wait for the traffic lights to change.

"Hurry up and change, lights," she shouted.

A lady with a briefcase looked at her. She saw the tears in Maggie's eyes.

"What's wrong?" she asked kindly. "Can I help you?"

"It's Sandy and the cat," cried Maggie, and she ran across the road. The lady ran after her.

27

They waited at the other side of
the bridge for five minutes, ten
minutes, fifteen minutes.
There was still no sign of Sandy and the cat.
"Don't give up," said the lady.
"I'll get a boat and have a look under
the bridge."
The lady jumped into the nearest
rowing boat and rowed under the bridge.
Maggie was crying so hard that she
couldn't see or hear a thing.

28

Suddenly Maggie heard a loud shout
from under the bridge.

"They're here – here – here," boomed
the lady's voice. "And they're all
right – right – right."

Maggie jumped up with joy and
wiped the tears from her eyes.
She couldn't wait for the lady to
come back with the boat.

Sandy was very tired. He couldn't
lift his head to look at Maggie.
He could only wag his tail a little.
The cat looked dead.

"There was a narrow ledge at the
side of the river under the bridge,"
said the lady.
"Sandy dragged himself and the cat onto
the ledge. He was too tired to go further."

Soon Sandy was feeling better, but
the cat still looked very bad.

The cat was very weak, but it lived. Sandy went to visit the cat every day. He gently licked her and after a few days she started to purr when she saw him. They became the best of friends.

"Your dog is a hero," said Mrs Macdonald, who loved her cat very much.

"He should get a medal," said Mr Macdonald, who also loved his cat very much.

Maggie and Sandy both agreed.

The lady who had helped Sandy and
the cat was a reporter.
She wrote a story about Sandy for the newspaper.
It was called "**FIRST PRIZE FOR SANDY**".

There was also a picture of Sandy in the
newspaper.

He was wearing a red ribbon which Mrs
Macdonald had made for him.
On the ribbon was a medal which Mr
Macdonald had made for him.
The medal said

**DOG HERO
FIRST CLASS**